THE LOST WORLD

RETOLD BY PAULINE FRANCIS

Evans

EVANS BROTHERS LIMITED

Published by Evans Brothers Limited
2A Portman Mansions
Chiltern Street
London W1U 6NR

© Evans Brothers Limited 2002
First published 2002

Printed in Hong Kong

British Library Cataloguing in Publication data.
Francis, Pauline
      The Lost World. – (Fast track classics)
      1. Children's stories
      I. Title II. Wells, H. G. (Herbert George), 1866-1946
      823.9'14 [J]
      ISBN 023752404X

THE LOST WORLD

Introduction

Arthur Conan Doyle was born in 1859, in Edinburgh, Scotland. When he left school, he spent a year in Austria before studying medicine at Edinburgh University. He had to learn how to diagnose illnesses, and he later used some of these methods in his Sherlock Holmes detective stories.

Conan Doyle set up in practice as a doctor in 1885, but he still needed to earn more money. He started to write detective stories for a magazine. Two years later, *A Study in Scarlet* was published. This story introduced the detective Sherlock Holmes for the first time. Holmes, and his friend Dr Watson, became so popular that Conan Doyle wrote more stories about them, including *The Hound of the Baskervilles.*

Conan Doyle was such a successful writer that he gave up his practice to write full time. Later in his career, he wrote scientific fiction featuring Professor Challenger – *The Lost World* (1912) and *The Poison Belt* (1913).

In *The Lost World*, Professor Challenger leads a scientific expedition to the Amazonian rain forest. The travellers are trapped on a plateau, in great danger from

dinosaurs and ape-men. The story of their struggle to escape is one of the most exciting adventure stories ever written. *The Lost World* was made into a film in 1925.

Sir Arthur Conan Doyle had many other interests apart from his writing – including the building of a Channel Tunnel. He died in 1930, at the age of seventy-one.

CHAPTER ONE
Professor Challenger

"Well, Mr Malone, for a man of only twenty-three, you seem very anxious to kill yourself!" Mr McArdle said.

Mr McArdle was the news editor of the *Daily Gazette*, in London, where I worked as a journalist.

"Oh no, sir," I replied, "I just want adventure, to make a name for myself. Is there something really exciting I can report on? The more difficult the better."

I did not tell him what my girlfriend had said the night before, when I had asked her to marry me.

"I'm sorry," Gladys had said, shaking her head, "I can only marry a brave man, a man who can look death in the face and not be afraid."

"I can't think of any..." Mr McArdle began. "No, just a minute! What about trying your luck with Professor Challenger?"

"The famous zoologist!" I cried. "But he's already fractured the skull of one of the reporters from the...!"

"You said you were after adventure," Mr McArdle smiled. "Professor Challenger went to South America two years ago. He came back full of stories about the strange animals he had seen there. Nobody believed him. Go and see what you can find out."

I wrote to Professor Challenger that same evening, pretending to be a scientist, asking for an interview. To my amazement, he agreed. When I arrived at his house, his wife met me at the door.

"I apologise to you in advance for my husband's behaviour," she said. "If he gets violent, leave the room immediately. Don't wait to argue with him. Do you want to talk to him about South America?"

I nodded.

"Oh dear!" she gasped. "That is his most dangerous subject. Pretend to believe him, or he may attack you."

Then Mrs Challenger tapped on the door of her husband's study and left me to enter the lion's cage. Her husband's appearance amazed me! He had an enormous head, the largest I have ever seen on a human being. He had a beard so black that it almost looked blue, and so long that it fell over his chest. Great black eyebrows sat over his blue-grey eyes. His chest was as big and round as a barrel.

"Well?" he bellowed at me. "I hope you are a scientist and not one of those revolting people who call themselves journalists."

He started to ask me questions and I agreed with everything he said.

"What does that prove?" Professor Challenger asked at last.

"Ah," I said, "what does that prove?"

"It proves that you are nothing but a vile, crawling journalist!" Challenger shouted. "You know nothing about science! I have been talking rubbish for the last ten minutes!"

Professor Challenger sprang to his feet, his eyes blazing with anger. To my surprise, I saw that he was very short. He began to walk towards me.

"Keep your hands off me, sir," I said, opening the door to the hall.

At that moment, he ran at me. We rolled through the door, along the hall and into the street through the front door, which the butler had thoughtfully opened.

"You bully!" I shouted, getting up at last.

A passing policeman came to help me, but I did not press charges. This pleased the professor and he asked me to return to the house. Back in his study, he swung round in his revolving chair and stared at me. Then he picked up a very tattered sketch-book.

"As you already know," he began, "I went to the River Amazon to examine the plants and animals. On my way back, I spent the night in an Indian village. To my surprise, I found another white man there. He had just died. His name was written in his knapsack – Maple White – and he was from the United States. This sketch-book was in his pocket. Take a look at it."

I turned over the pages until I came to a painting of the most extraordinary creature I had ever seen. Its head was like a chicken's, its body like a bloated lizard's, with a trailing tail full of spikes. It was taller than a railway station.

"It's horrible," I said, shuddering. "What is it?"

"A stegosaurus," the Professor said.

"Did Maple White copy it from a book?" I asked.

Professor Challenger did not answer my question, but he handed me a faded photograph. It showed a long, high cliff dotted with trees — exactly the same as the background of the painting. On the top of one of the trees stood a strange bird.

"I shot a bird like that two years ago," the Professor told me, "but unfortunately, I lost it in the river when my boat overturned. But I managed to save this…"

He opened a drawer and took out part of a huge wing.

"Is it a pelican, or a bat?" I asked.

"No, my young friend," he said.

The Professor leaned across his desk towards me.

"It is a pterodactyl," he said. "A flying dinosaur. It lived more than a hundred and fifty million years ago. And it's still alive in South America today."

CHAPTER TWO
Journey to South America

I believed Professor Challenger.

"You've discovered a lost world!" I cried, "and I'm sorry that nobody believes you."

"I have been invited to speak at the Zoological Institute this evening," the Professor said. "Why don't you come along? Then you can see for yourself how the public dislikes me."

It was true! I had never heard a man so insulted as Professor Challenger was that evening. A man called Professor Summerlee was the worst of all. He rose to his feet, cheered on by the audience.

"And where exactly did you see these dinosaurs?" he asked coldly.

There was a long silence. Then Professor Challenger walked to the front of the platform and stared at Professor Summerlee.

"I will take you there!" he shouted. "Will you come?"

"Yes!" Professor Summerlee shouted back.

"I will need a younger man to go with us!" Professor Challenger called to the audience. "Are there any volunteers here?"

For a second, I thought of what Gladys had said.

"I'll go with you!" I shouted, jumping to my feet.

"And so will I!" another man said.

The voice came from a tall, thin man standing a few rows in front of me.

"Your name, sir?" Professor Challenger asked him.

"I am Lord John Roxton," the man replied. "I have already travelled to the Amazon."

And so our fate was decided. My newspaper agreed to let me go to South America on condition that I sent regular reports back to the *Daily Gazette.*

Our ship left England on a foggy morning in late spring. After many weeks at sea, we went by steam-ship to the River Amazon. On the second of August, we started our journey up the Amazon by canoe.

There were thick woods on either side of the river, and the professors told me all the names of the trees. Bright flowers peeped out everywhere from climbing creepers. At the river level, there was no animal life anywhere, but high above our heads in the bright sunshine, we heard the chatter of monkeys and the call of birds. As we travelled deeper into the Amazonian jungle, we heard the beating of Indian drums.

The time came when we had to leave this fairyland. We hid our canoes under some bushes, put our belongings in our rucksacks, and started to climb away from the river.

"The plateau we are going to was pushed high into the air during a volcanic eruption," Professor Challenger told us, "at a time when dinosaurs still lived. The cliffs around it are made of granite, so hard that they have not crumbled. The plateau, and all its wild life, has been cut off from the rest of the continent ever since."

We climbed for nine days, through trees and tall bamboo, which cut out all the sunlight from above. At last, we came out into the open again, near the foot of a row of hills. As we came closer to the hills, Professor Challenger suddenly pointed upwards.

"Did you see it?" he shouted. "Summerlee, did you see it?"

"No," Summerlee replied. "What do you claim it was?"

"A pterodactyl," Professor Challenger said firmly.

Professor Summerlee started to laugh.

"A ptero-fiddlesticks!" he said.

Professor Challenger was too angry to speak. He simply picked up his rucksack and walked on. Lord John caught up with me.

"I saw the creature through my binoculars," he whispered. "I can honestly say that I've never seen a creature like it, not in my whole life."

We carried on walking. Then, suddenly, in the distance, I saw a line of tall red cliffs, like the ones in Maple White's painting.

"The plateau!" I gasped. "Look! We're there, at last!"

I am looking at the cliffs, Mr McArdle, as I write this letter to you. I will send this letter, and a rough map, with one of the Indians who has cut his arm badly on the bamboo and cannot go with us any further.

I wonder if you will ever hear from me again? Tomorrow we go into an unknown world – the lost world.

CHAPTER THREE
The Lost World

I am going to carry on writing this down but I am now afraid that nobody will ever read what I have written. We may have to stay here in the lost world for ever! I am so confused that I can hardly think clearly…a terrible thing has happened…

We started to walk towards the cliffs as soon as I had finished writing my last letter. These cliffs were at least one thousand feet high, with thick trees growing at the top. That night, we set up our tent right under them.

"You see that rock up there," Professor Challenger said. "That's where I shot the pterodactyl two years ago."

To my surprise, Professor Summerlee did not sneer. In fact, for the first time, a look of excitement passed over his face.

"I could not climb these cliffs up to the plateau on my last visit," Challenger said, "I had no ropes long enough, and the rainy season was starting. You can see that the cliff above us overhangs so much that we shall have to climb it from another spot. It is possible. Maple White did it. That is where he saw the stegosaurus."

"I admit that your plateau now exists," Professor Summerlee said. "But I am not yet satisfied that it contains any form of prehistoric life."

We walked westwards, looking for a place to climb the cliff. We came across the remains of a camp, and this cheered us up.

"It's not my old camp," Professor Challenger said. "It must be Maple White's. Look, there is a mark on that tree, pointing west. This is the way he must have gone."

We walked on until we reached a clump of bamboo, twenty feet high, with tips as sharp as spears. Suddenly, I caught sight of something white inside the clump. I looked down and found myself gazing at a skeleton.

"Every bone in his body is broken," Lord John said sadly. "I wonder who he is?"

"Maple White was travelling with a friend," Professor Challenger said. "The Indians told me. This might be him."

"He must have fallen from the top of the cliff," Lord John said, "or been pushed."

We moved on in silence, following Maple White's arrows. At last, hungry and tired, we came to a narrow cave in the cliff, about forty feet across, with more white arrows on its walls.

We crawled, one by one, to the back of the cave. Suddenly, Lord John stopped.

"It's blocked!" he shouted. "The roof has fallen in!"

We stumbled back through the narrow tunnel, too

tired and too disappointed to talk. Then we made our way back to the camp and lit a fire to cook a meal.

As we sat eating, we heard a loud swish in the darkness. We looked up and saw huge, leathery wings hovering above our heads. I glimpsed a long, snake-like neck, a great snapping beak filled with gleaming teeth. The next moment, it was gone – and so was our dinner. A huge, black shadow, about twenty feet across, rose into the air. For a moment, the monster's wings blotted out the stars, then vanished over the edge of the cliff above us.

"Professor Challenger," Professor Summerlee said in a trembling voice, "I owe you an apology and I beg you to forgive me."

For the first time, the two men shook hands.

We spent six more days walking round the whole edge of the plateau looking for a way up, with no success. But one morning, Professor Challenger greeted us at breakfast with a wide smile. He pointed to the peak of a rock above our tents.

"I think I have solved the problem," he said. "I want you all to climb to the top of that rock with me."

When we had climbed the rock, we saw that we were level with the plateau. It looked so close that I almost put out my hand to touch it – but there was a deep gorge between us.

"It's only forty feet across, but it may as well be forty miles," I said, clinging onto a large tree as I looked.

Professor Challenger stared at the tree and smiled.

"A bridge!" Lord John exclaimed. "So that's what you had in mind!"

It was easy! Our Indian guides cut down the tree and it fell across the gorge. Then we walked over on it, one by one. Soon all four of us were in that dreamland, in that lost world.

But as we gazed around at the plateau, a loud crash came from behind us and made us jump. We turned round.

The tree had disappeared.

CHAPTER FOUR

The Iguanodon Glade

We rushed to the edge of the gorge and stared down in horror. Right at the bottom of the cliff I saw a tangled mass of branches and a splintered tree trunk.

"At least our guides are still on the other side," Professor Challenger said. "They can help us. That will give us time to think about our situation."

"It's hopeless!" I thought. "Hopeless!"

The Indian guides threw a rope to us, and all day long, we pulled crates of food and guns across the gorge.

"This will keep us going for a week," Professor Challenger muttered, "until we find a way back."

The next morning, we began our new life on the plateau. We moved our food and our rifles to a small clearing surrounded by trees on all sides and placed thorny bushes around them. We called it Fort Challenger.

"For the minute, we are safe," Lord John said cheerfully. "There is no evidence that man or beast has spotted us. We must spy out the land before we decide on a course of action. We must always be able to get back to Fort Challenger and never fire our guns unless it is a matter of life or death."

He turned to me.

"You will draw a map as we go, Malone," Lord John said. "What shall we call this land?"

"Maple White Land," Professor Challenger boomed, "after the man who discovered it."

I wrote down the name on my map. Then we set off into the unknown. We had hardly gone more than a few yards when we came to a large marsh. Lord John, who was leading us, put out a hand to stop us.

"Look at this!" he called.

In the soft mud was an enormous, three-toed footprint.

"It's fresh," Lord John said.

"There's another print," Professor Summerlee called. "It looks like a huge human hand."

"I've seen it before," Professor Challenger said, excited. "It's a dinosaur. Nothing else leaves such a track. It walks on three-toed feet and puts down its five-fingered paw from time to time."

We walked on through a small wood and came out into a clearing beyond it. Here were five of the most extraordinary creatures I had ever seen, their skin slate-coloured and scaly like a lizard's. They looked like monstrous kangaroos, twenty feet in length. They had made the footprints.

I do not know how long we stood looking at those amazing creatures. I glanced at my friends. Lord John stared, his finger on the trigger of his gun. The two Professors were so excited by what they saw that they had grabbed hold of each other's arm as they watched, smiling like two little children.

"Put this in your diary, Malone," Lord John whispered.

"What are they?" I asked.

"Iguanodons," Professor Summerlee said. "You'll find their fossil footprints all over the south of England."

I was excited, too, but at the same time I felt a strange feeling of mystery and danger all around us. The gloom of the trees looked threatening. What horrors might the thick foliage hold? What fierce creatures might pounce on us?

The dangers I feared were not long in coming.

CHAPTER FIVE
A Thousand Pterodactyls

We passed very slowly through the woods again, moving only when Lord John waved us on. After about two or three miles, we came to another opening in the trees, and clumps of waist-high bushes leading up to some large boulders.

A strange sound filled the air, like a soft whistling, which seemed to come from in front of us. We crept up to the rocks and peered over them. We were staring down into a large pit filled with stagnant water − and about a thousand pterodactyls.

The males perched on rocks above the water - tall, grey and withered-looking. They sat absolutely still, except for the rolling of their red eyes, or the snap of their beaks as a dragonfly flew past. Their wings were folded around their shoulders like grey shawls.

The Professors became so excited that Professor Challenger thrust his head above the rock. The nearest male gave a shrill, whistling cry and flapped its twenty-foot long wing. Then it soared into the air, followed by all the males. It was a wonderful and terrifying sight. The creatures swooped like swallows, flying lower and lower and filling the air with a deafening sound.

"Make for the woods and keep together!" Lord John
cried. "These brutes mean trouble!"

As we ran, a beak stabbed at us. Then another, and
another. Professor Summerlee gave a cry as blood ran
down his face. Professor Challenger fell over and I
stooped to pick him up. A beak struck the back of my
neck and I fell on top of him. Lord John fired his gun and
broke one of the creature's wings. It struggled along the
ground, spitting and gurgling, its beak wide-open.

"Run!" Lord John cried, "run!"

We were safe in the woods because there was no space for the creatures' huge wings. As we limped back to camp, we saw them for a long time, flying high in the sky, their eyes following us all the time. But as we reached the thicker woods, they gave up and flew away.

"A most interesting experience," Professor Challenger said, as he bathed his swollen knee. "Now we know all there is to know about an angry pterodactyl."

There was an even greater surprise for us back at Fort Challenger. Tins of meat had been crushed and gun cartridges had been smashed to pieces. We gazed around with frightened eyes, wondering who might be lurking in the trees.

Professor Summerlee and I slept most of the day, feverish from the pterodactyls' bites. From time to time, I was sure that somebody was watching me. And that night, all of us were woken up by terrible screams close to the camp. I had never heard a sound like it – full of agony and horror. A cold sweat broke out over my body, and I felt sick as I listened to it.

These sounds continued for three or four minutes, then stopped suddenly. For a long time we sat in horrified silence. Then Professor Summerlee raised his hand.

"Sssh…" he said. "I can hear something."

From the deep silence came a pitter-patter, like the footsteps of an animal. It circled the camp, then stopped at the gate. We could hear heavy breathing. I peered through a hole in the hedge. In the deep shadows, I saw a deep crouching shape. It was no higher than a horse, but bulkier. It moved and I thought I saw the glint of green eyes.

Lord John picked up a blazing branch from the fire and ran at the animal. For one moment, I glimpsed its terrifying face, its flabby mouth dripping with blood. Then there was a great crash and our visitor disappeared into the bushes.

In the morning, we found out the meaning of those hideous noises the night before. The iguanodon glade was a scene of horrible butchery. Pools of blood and enormous lumps of flesh were scattered in every direction, but all from one body.

"The creature we saw last night must have done this," Lord John said.

Professor Challenger examined the teeth marks on the torn flesh.

"A flesh-eating dinosaur, I think," he said, laughing with excitement. "Perhaps an allosaurus."

"Or a megalosaurus," Professor Summerlee shouted.

His face suddenly became serious.

"This plateau is dangerous," he said, "we should be

thinking of finding a way back. I have all the proof I need."

"I refuse to leave before we have made a decent exploration of this country," Professor Challenger said. "We must go back with a complete map."

"That will take months!" Professor Summerlee protested.

I suddenly had an idea.

"Look!" I said, "we're sitting right under the tallest tree I've ever seen! I'm a skilled tree-climber. Let me go to the top. I'll be able to see the whole plateau from there."

"Well done, young fellow!" Lord John said, slapping me on the back. "Why didn't we think of it before? Come on, there's about one hour of daylight left."

I stood under the tree, ready. Professor Challenger pushed me so hard with his huge hands that I shot right up into its branches. I climbed quickly, and soon even Challenger's booming voice became faint.

I came to a thick clump of leaves tied to a branch. I stopped for a moment to look at it before I climbed on. But I nearly fell from the branch with shock.

A face was gazing back at me.

CHAPTER SIX
The Ape-men

The face in front of me was long and pale, with wild eyes. Whiskers grew on its pointed jaw. The creature looked more like a human than a monkey. As I tried to move, it opened its mouth and snarled at me. Then it disappeared into the foliage.

"Did you see it?" I shouted down to the others, "did you see it? An ape-man!"

I decided to go on climbing, although I was nervous at the thought. The sun was low in the west when I reached the top of the tree. I held my breath in excitement as I gazed at the view. I could see the whole plateau in front of me!

At its centre was a huge lake, sparkling green and beautiful in the evening light. At its edges lay long dark objects – too large for alligators and too long for canoes. I took out my spy-glass to look at them more closely – they were animals I did not recognise.

I could see the iguanodon glade, the pterodactyl

swamp, and in the distant red cliffs a number of dark holes – the mouths of caves. I sat sketching my map until the sun had set. Then I climbed down again, and for once, I was the hero of the day. Everybody shook my hand.

"The ape-man has been there all the time," I told them. "I knew that somebody was watching us."

"There is no such thing as an ape-man," Professor Challenger said.

"Isn't there?" I thought, smiling to myself, "he looked very much like you, sir!"

"Of course, the creature could be what we scientists call 'the missing link' between man and monkey," Challenger said.

"Nonsense!" Professor Summerlee said, "there's no such thing! And now that we have our map of the plateau, let us look for a way out of this awful place."

I worked on the map until late into the night.

"Why not give the lake your name?" Professor Challenger said. "You saw it first."

"I should like to call it Lake Gladys," I replied, blushing.

Professor Challenger looked at me with some sympathy.

"Boys will be boys," he smiled. "Let it be Lake Gladys then."

As you will have noticed, I was the youngest and least experienced member of this expedition, and I glowed with pride after my descent from the tree. At last, I felt that I was becoming a man and I felt more confident.

But I let it go to my head! That night, I had the worst experience of my life, a night that makes me feel sick every time I think about it.

I was so excited by the events of the day that I could not sleep. Everybody else was asleep, although Professor Summerlee was supposed to be on guard. The moon was out and the air was crisp and cold.

"What a wonderful night for a walk!" I thought.

The idea went round and round in my head. What if I went down to the lake? In the morning, I would be a hero again. Think what this would do for my career! And think how proud Gladys would be of me!

I slipped quietly out of the camp. I had only gone about a hundred yards when I regretted what I had done. It was dreadful in the forest. The trees were so thick that I could not see the moon. I thought all the time of the terrible cry of the iguanodon as it died, of the terrible creature that had killed it. Now I was on its hunting-ground!

I began to tremble with fear. That nameless and horrible monster could jump out at me at any moment.

CHAPTER SEVEN

Danger at Lake Gladys

I reached the open glade of the iguanodons. To my relief, it was deserted, and I slipped rapidly across it into the jungle on the other side. I came alongside a stream, leading down to Lake Gladys.

I passed close to the pterodactyl swamp. One of the creatures took to the air as I passed, and the moonlight light shone through its wings. It looked like a flying skeleton. I crouched in the bushes, knowing that with one cry, it could bring hundreds of its horrible friends to fight me. When it had landed again, I went on my way.

It was a terrifying walk. I kept stopping to hide whenever wild animals went by. Enormous, silent shadows seemed to be prowling all around me and I did not know if they were real or not.

At about one o' clock in the morning, I reached the lake. I climbed up onto a rock and looked across at the red cliffs. I could see the caves clearly now, and lights shining from them.

"Fires!" I gasped. "So there are human beings here! How right I was to come down to the lake! What news I have to tell the others, and everybody in London!"

As I sat watching, an enormous animal began to make its way down to the edge of the water. The ground trembled under its weight. It drank from the lake, so close to me that I could have touched it. Where had I seen it before? I stared at its tiny head close to the ground, at its arched back with triangular fringe – it was a stegosaurus, the creature that Maple White had painted.

As the dinosaur lumbered away, I set off back to the camp. I was plodding up the slope towards the stream, feeling very pleased with myself, when I heard a strange noise behind me - like a snore or a low growl. I walked more quickly. The noise became louder and closer. My heart almost stopped beating.

"It's following me!" I thought.

My skin went cold. With my knees shaking, I turned to look at the moonlit path behind me. It was empty. Then I heard the noise again. I stood still, paralysed with fear. Then, suddenly, I saw it. A great dark shadow jumped into the moonlight. It had the broad flat toad-like face of the monster I had seen outside our camp!

"A flesh-eating dinosaur!" I gasped, "the most terrible beast that has ever lived on the earth!"

I ran faster than I had ever run in my life. My legs ached, I could hardly breathe, but with that horror behind me, I ran and ran. At last, I paused, hardly able to move. For I moment I thought that the creature had gone. Then, suddenly, with a crashing and a thudding of giant feet, the beast was just behind me again. Now he hunted by sight, not by scent.

The moonlight shone on the creature's huge eyes, the row of enormous teeth in his open mouth and on his gleaming claws. I expected to feel his teeth on my back at every moment. Suddenly, I heard a loud crash and I was falling through space. I lost consciousness.

A few minutes later, I opened my eyes. I put out my hand and felt an enormous piece of meat or flesh. Then I looked at the walls around me.

"I've fallen into a pit!" I gasped.

I got up and walked around. In the middle of the pit was a tall post, its sharp end blackened by the blood of animals that had fallen onto it.

"I must get out!" I thought. "I don't think the creature will be waiting for me up there. It's not very intelligent. Out of sight, out of mind."

I managed to climb out of the pit and I walked on as the sun began to rise. Suddenly, I heard the shot of a rifle from the direction of Fort Challenger.

"The others must have discovered that I'm not there," I thought. "They think I'm lost in the woods and they're sending me a signal."

When I was close to the camp, I shouted a greeting so that my friends would not be afraid. There was no reply. I started to run until I reached the gates. Then I rushed inside, my heart sinking.

A terrible sight met my eyes in that cold morning light. Our possessions were scattered everywhere and the fire had gone out. But worst of all, my friends were not there.

And on the grass was an enormous pool of blood.

CHAPTER EIGHT
Saving the Professors

I was so shocked by what I saw that I almost went mad. All day long I rushed around the wood calling wildly for my friends. There was no answer. What if I never saw them again? What if I was left alone in this dreadful place? What if I died in this nightmare country? Without my friends, I was like a child in the dark, helpless and powerless.

"There was only one shot," I thought when I became calmer. "The attack must have been very quick and it happened just before I arrived. There's some food left, and the guns are still here. They must have been attacked by an animal, not a human being."

That night, I was so tired that I fell into a deep sleep. Just as dawn was breaking, a hand touched my arm. I woke up with a jump and reached for my rifle.

"Lord John!" I cried, looking at the man kneeling next to me.

How different he was! Now his eyes were wild and his face was pale and blood-stained. He breathed heavily as if he had run for miles. His clothes hung in rags and his hat was missing.

"Quick, Malone!" he said, "every minute counts! Get

the rifles and some bullets! Fill your pockets. Take some food. Don't talk or think. Hurry up, or we're dead."

I ran after him into the wood, half-asleep, until we came to a thick clump of thorn bushes. Lord John hid behind them, pulling me in after him.

"Who's after us?" I asked.

"The ape-men!" he whispered. "My God, what brutes they are! Speak quietly because they have good hearing, but no sense of smell."

"What happened yesterday?" I asked.

"It suddenly rained apes," he told me. "They came down from the trees above us, as thick as apples."

"I heard a shot," I said.

"I killed one of them." Lord John said, "but they were too strong for us. "The missing link, eh? I wish they'd stayed missing."

He sighed.

"They just sat and looked at us. Murder was in their eyes. Even Challenger was afraid. But he managed to bellow at them, cursing them and shouting. I thought they'd kill us there and then."

"Why didn't they?" I whispered.

"They talked for a long time. Then one of them, their chief I realised later, came and stood next to Challenger. Malone, you wouldn't have believed it! Their chief was a sort of...red-haired Challenger. He had the same short body, the big shoulders, the round chest, great wavy beard, tufted eyebrows. It was amazing! The ape-man put his paw on Challenger's shoulder. Then four ape-men came forward and carried Challenger on their shoulders. They just dragged me and Summerlee."

"Where to?" I asked.

"To their town," he explained, "about three or four miles away. They've built about a thousand huts of branches and leaves in the trees on the red cliffs."

Lord John shuddered.

"I've learned something that will interest you," he said. "The ape-men control this side of the plateau, the Indians in the caves control the other. It's war all the time between them. Yesterday, the ape-men captured a dozen Indians. Killed two of them straight away."

Lord John wiped his face with a trembling hand.

"Do you remember that body we found in the bamboo at the bottom of the cliff, Maple White's friend?"

I nodded.

"It's just below ape-town," he said. "That's where they play their game."

"Game?" I gasped.

"They line up their prisoners and make them jump off the cliff," Lord John said. "The game is to see if they land on top of the sharp bamboo or not. They made us watch. Four of the Indians jumped and the cane went through them like knitting needles."

I felt sick as he told me.

"They're saving six of the Indians for today...and then...who knows? They'll probably kill Summerlee. They might let Challenger live."

I had almost forgotten about the Professors.

"Why aren't they with you?" I asked.

"Challenger was still up in the tree with the ape-men when I ran away," Lord John said, "and Summerlee was too frightened to follow me. I thought our best chance was to find you and get the guns. We have go back now. Let us hope we are not too late."

We set off for ape-town at once. It was a sight I shall never forget to my dying day. Round a clearing near the edge of the cliffs were the ape-houses, built in the trees, crowded with the females and the children. In the open, near the edge of the cliff, stood about a hundred of these red-haired creatures, all of them enormous and horrible to look at. In front of them stood a group of Indians — and next to them, Professor Summerlee.

Professor Challenger stood next to the chief, looking as wild as the ape-men.

Suddenly, the chief raised his hand. Two ape-men dragged one of the Indians to the edge of the cliff and swung him three times. He vanished from our sight as

they let go. The ape-men cheered. Then they dragged
Professor Summerlee forward.

"Come on!" Lord John whispered frantically. "Run
forward. I'll take a shot at the chief!"

As the chief fell to the ground, Professor Challenger
realised what was happening. He ran and caught hold of
Professor Summerlee, dragging him towards us. We gave
them a rifle each. Then we ran for our lives, followed by
the Indian prisoners.

And with a tremendous roar of anger, the ape-men
ran after us.

CHAPTER NINE

The Battle of the Ape-men

The ape-men gave up the chase as soon as they found out that our guns would kill them. We managed to reach the camp without one of them in sight.

"You've pulled us from the jaws of death!" Professor Summerlee laughed. "A good bit of work!"

"Yes," Professor Challenger boomed. "Not only the two of us, but the whole world of science is in your debt for what you have done. The disappearance of myself and Professor Summerlee would have left a huge gap in zoological history."

"Well, it's lucky that you look like them," Lord John said, "otherwise, we might all have been killed on the spot yesterday."

"Let us change the subject," Challenger said quickly. "The question we have to answer is, what are we going to do with these Indians? We can't take them home because we don't know where they live."

"They live in caves on the other side of the lake," I said proudly, "about twenty miles away."

Professor Summerlee groaned.

"We'll never get there with these brutes on our tracks."

As he spoke, the cry of the ape-men came from the woods. We took everything from our camp and ran to hide in the bushes. All day long we heard them calling, but none came in our direction. We began to feel safe again.

Why did we forget so quickly how cunning and how patient the ape-men were? The next morning, they killed one of the Indians who had gone to fetch water from the stream. When I found him, I called out a warning to the others in the camp.

As I bent over the body, I heard a rustle of leaves in the tree above me, and I looked up. Out of the foliage came two long muscular arms, covered with reddish hair.

I jumped backwards, but one of the hands caught the back of my neck, and the other one my face. I was lifted from the ground. My head began to spin as I tried to pull the hands away. I stared at the ape-man's cold blue eyes. I stopped struggling. As soon as he felt this, the creature tightened his grip and bared his teeth at me. I heard the crack of a rifle and felt myself falling to the ground.

"You've had the escape of your life, young fellow," Lord John said as I opened my eyes. "They're watching us on all sides. Our only hope is to make for the lake and take the Indians home."

We started our journey in the afternoon. We heard the yells of the ape-men, but they did not come after us as we left the trees behind. When we reached the lake, a wonderful sight met us – as far as the eye could see, canoes full of Indians glided over the shimmering water.

It was clear from their talk that the Indians had decided to attack the ape-men, whom they hated as much as we did. They wanted to have a future free from their violence.

"They want us to help them," Lord John said. "I'm keen, are you?"

Professor Challenger and I nodded.

"That was not the point of this expedition," Professor Summerlee said. "But if you are all going to fight, I shall have to come with you."

During the night, more Indians came across the lake to join us. And in the first light of day, about five hundred of us were ready to fight. We did not have to wait long for our enemy. As we walked from the lake towards the forest, a wild yelling rose from the trees. A group of ape-men rushed towards us, waving sticks and stones.

The battle did not last long. The ape-men were slow on their feet and the Indians were nimble. Arrow after arrow hit the ape-men and we only had to use our guns once. It was more dangerous when we entered the trees. We fought here for more than an hour, until the creatures suddenly panicked and ran back to ape-town.

We ran after them, firing bullets and arrows, until the last ape-men, about forty of them, stood at the edge of the cliff. Some died where they stood, others threw themselves over onto the sharp bamboo hundreds of feet below.

"It's over," Lord John said at last. "On this plateau, in Maple White Land, the future belongs to man."

"We have had enough adventures," Professor Summerlee said. "From now on, we must give all our energy to getting out of this horrible country and back to civilization."

CHAPTER TEN
Prfessor Challenger's Surprise

We went back with the Indians to their caves. But they did not try to help us to leave the plateau. I do not know why, perhaps they felt safer with us. Or perhaps they did not want us to come back with more white men.

It was the chief's son, one of the Indians we had rescued from the ape-men, who decided to help us. He came to our little camp one night and gave us a small roll of tree bark. He quickly pointed to a row of caves above our heads and went back to his own people.

We opened the scroll and saw charcoal marks on it, one with a cross below it.

"Eighteen marks!" Lord John said, "and there are eighteen caves up there. The cross marks the cave we must take. If it's deep enough, it will take us a long way down inside the cliff. We can use our rope to go down the rest of the way."

And that is what we did! We left everything behind, so that the Indians would not notice that we had gone – everything except an enormous package that Professor Challenger kept with him all the time.

And so I finish this humble account of our adventures in the lost world. Tomorrow we begin our journey back to England…

Amazing scenes at meeting of the Zoological Institute!

Nobody is ever likely to forget the sensation caused by Professor Challenger at last night's meeting, which was attended by five thousand people.

You will remember that Professor Challenger returned to the Amazon earlier this year to bring back proof that dinosaurs were still alive there.

At the end of the talk, a Dr Illingworth, from Edinburgh University, stood up to ask a question.

"May I ask what proof there is?" he demanded. "A few photographs and sketches, which may be all fakes!"

Professor Challenger got to his feet.

"I remember similar scenes at the meeting last year," he said. "Then it was Professor Summerlee who caused all the trouble. He knows better now. Many of our photographs were destroyed when the ape-men attacked our camp. And we had to leave most of our things behind when we escaped."

Loud laughter stopped the Professor's speech for a few seconds.

"I do have a photograph of a pterodactyl," Professor Challenger shouted above the noise.

"No photograph would convince us!" Dr Illingworth laughed.

"What if you could see one, would you believe me then?" Challenger asked.

Dr Illingworth and the audience laughed louder.

"Certainly!" Dr Illingworth replied.

It was at this point that the sensation of the evening took place – a sensation so dramatic that nothing like it has ever happened in the history of scientific meetings.

Professor Challenger raised his hand as a signal and a journalist on this newspaper, Mr Malone, made his way to the back of the platform. Then he dragged a large packing-case over to Professor Challenger's chair.

The audience fell silent as the Professor opened the lid of the box. He peered into it, snapping his fingers several times. A moment later, with a scratching and a rattling, the most horrible creature I have ever seen emerged.

The face of the creature was evil and horrible, with red eyes as bright as fire. Its long mouth was half-open, showing two rows of sharp teeth. Its shoulders were hunched and draped with grey, like an old shawl.

It was the devil of our childhood sitting in front of us.

People began to scream. Two ladies in the front row fainted. Professor Challenger put up his hands to try to quieten his audience, but this movement alarmed the creature next to him.

47

Its strange shawl slowly unfurled, spreading out long, leathery wings. It sprang from its perch and circled round the hall, sending a terrible smell everywhere. Those glowing eyes and murderous beak sent everyone into a panic. Faster and faster it flew, beating its wings against the walls and the chandeliers.

"Shut the window!" Professor Challenger bellowed.

But his warning came too late. In a second, the hideous creature squeezed through it and was gone.

Professor Challenger fell back in his chair and buried his face in his hands. But the audience started to clap and cheer. Then they carried the four heroes out into the street, singing and shouting.

And so ended one of the most remarkable evenings that London has ever seen.

And the pterodactyl? It was last seen flying over the Atlantic Ocean.

I want to add a few last words to my story. Gladys married somebody else while I was away in South America. But soon, Lord John Roxford and I set sail again – for Maple White Land.